This *LADYBIRD TALE*
belongs to

....

The Emperor's New Clothes

Retold by Lynne Bradbury
with illustrations by Valentina Belloni

LADYBIRD  TALES

LONG AGO, THERE LIVED an emperor who *loved* new clothes. He had clothes for the morning and he had different clothes for the afternoon. He also had special clothes for the evening.

One day, two wicked men came to the town.

"We make cloth," said one man.

"Yes, we are weavers," said the other man.

"We can make very special cloth," said both men together.

The emperor was very pleased. He wanted some new cloth to make a special new suit of clothes.

"Tell me about your special cloth," said the emperor.

The weavers told the emperor that their cloth was so special that anyone who couldn't see it must be very stupid. The emperor was even more pleased.

The weavers wanted to start work. "We need gold thread," they said.

The emperor gave them lots and lots of gold thread to make their special cloth.

But the wicked weavers stole the gold thread. They hid it in their bags.

Then they pretended to make the special cloth. The weavers worked very hard. The loom that made cloth went backwards and forwards. *Click, clack, click, clack,* it went.

One night, the emperor wanted to know if the gold cloth was ready. He sent his prime minister to have a look.

"Come and tell me if the cloth is beautiful," ordered the emperor.

The prime minister went to
see the weavers. They were
working very hard. *Click, clack,
click, clack*, went the loom. The
prime minister looked and looked.

"Oh dear!" he thought.
"I can't see anything.
But *I* am not stupid."

So he said to the weavers,
"It's beautiful cloth. I'll tell
the emperor."

When he had gone, the weavers laughed and laughed. Then they said, "We need some more gold thread to make this special cloth."

The emperor let them have lots more gold thread. The wicked weavers stole the thread and hid it in their bags.

Then they worked harder than ever. *Click, clack, click, clack, click*, went the loom.

The prime minister told the emperor that the cloth was very beautiful. Soon, everyone was talking about the emperor's new suit.

The next night, the emperor
wanted someone else to look at the
cloth for his new suit. This time
he sent the captain of the guard.

"Come and tell me if it is
finished," ordered the emperor.

The captain went to see the weavers. They were still working very hard. *Click, clack, click, clack, click,* went the loom.

The captain looked and looked. "Oh dear!" he thought. "I can't see anything. But the prime minister could see the cloth and *I* am not stupid."

The captain told the weavers, "It's beautiful cloth. The emperor will be pleased. I'll tell him."

When he had gone, the weavers laughed and laughed. Then they worked faster and faster.

Soon the weavers said that the special cloth was made. They pretended to cut the cloth into pieces and sew them together to make the emperor's new clothes.

The next day the weavers said,
"Please can the emperor come and
try on his new suit? Then we can
finish the sewing."

The emperor was very pleased.
He went to see the weavers.

"Oh dear! I can't see the cloth!"
said the emperor, to himself.
"The prime minister and the
captain of the guard could see it.
I am not stupid." So the emperor
said, "This is beautiful cloth. These
will be my very best clothes."

Now it was time to try on his suit. The weavers made the emperor take off his clothes. Then he had to stand still. The weavers made sure that the new suit would fit the emperor.

He felt cold but he said, "This will be a beautiful suit of clothes. The cloth is so light that I can hardly feel it."

When the emperor had gone,
the weavers laughed and laughed.
They said they must sew faster
and faster so that the new clothes
would be finished.

Everyone in the land had heard
about the new suit. In two days
there was going to be a parade
in the town and the emperor was
going to wear his new clothes.
Everyone would be there to
see him.

At the end of the next day, the weavers said that the new suit of clothes was finished. Everyone went to look.

The prime minister said, "It's a wonderful new suit."

And the captain of the guard said, "I have never seen such beautiful clothes."

Then came the day of the parade. The weavers helped the emperor to dress. They made sure his suit was just right and then they put his crown on his head.

"Your majesty, you look wonderful!" said the weavers. And the emperor gave the weavers two big bags of gold.

The emperor was very, very pleased with his new clothes.

"All the people will look at me," he said to himself. He went out to join the parade.

The people of the town had hung flags from their houses. They stood at the sides of the roads waiting for the emperor to pass by.

Then the parade started and all the people began to shout and wave.

Everyone had heard about the special cloth. They had been told that only stupid people could not see it.

"The emperor's new clothes are beautiful," said one man.

"Doesn't he look wonderful!" said an old woman.

"This is a very special suit," said another man.

"Yes! Yes!" shouted all the people.

The emperor was very happy. "These are the best clothes I've ever had," he said.

He laughed and waved to all the people and they waved back at him.

The parade was nearly finished. The emperor thought that it had been the best day of his life.

Then, suddenly, a little boy pointed at the emperor. The boy began to laugh. "The emperor has nothing on!" he shouted.

And all the people began to laugh, too.

The emperor knew that he had been tricked. "I am very stupid," he thought. His cheeks went very, very red.

Of course, the weavers had gone!

A History of
The Emperor's
New Clothes

The Emperor's New Clothes, featuring two weavers who play a confidence trick on a vain emperor, is probably one of Hans Christian Andersen's best-loved stories.

It first appeared alongside *The Little Mermaid* as the third and final instalment of Andersen's *Fairy Tales Told for Children* in 1837.

Andersen's tale was based on the German translation of a medieval Spanish story. *The Emperor's New Clothes* has since gained such popularity that the phrase 'the emperor's new clothes' is often used to refer to anything silly and pompous.

Hans Christian Andersen changed the ending of the story to have the little boy laughing at the emperor – this might be the reason this version of the tale is all the more appealing to children.

Ladybird's 1980 retelling of *The Emperor's New Clothes* retains all the humour of the original story, albeit tailored for a modern audience.

Collect more fantastic

LADYBIRD 🐞 TALES

Little Red Riding Hood

9781409311126

Goldilocks and the Three Bears

9781409311119

Cinderella

9781409311072

Jack and the Beanstalk

9781409311102

The Gingerbread Man

9781409311096

The Three Little Pigs

9781409311089

The Three Billy Goats Gruff

9781409311065

Hansel and Gretel

9781409311133

Puss in Boots

9781409311225

Rapunzel

9781409311195

Rumpelstiltskin

9781409311164

The Elves and the Shoemaker

9781409311188

Snow White and the Seven Dwarfs

9781409311171

The Enormous Turnip

9781409311218

The Magic Porridge Pot

9781409311201

Sleeping Beauty

9781409311157

The Princess and the Frog

9780718192556

Dick Whittington

9780718192532

The Big Pancake

9780718192549

Beauty and the Beast

9780718192587

The Little Red Hen

9780718192525

The Ugly Duckling

9780718193133

The Princess and the Pea

9780718192570

Chicken Licken

9780718192563

The Emperor's New Clothes

9780723271048

The Little Mermaid

9780723271055

Pinocchio

9780723271062

Aladdin

9780723271079

Endpapers taken from series 606d,
first published in 1964

A catalogue record for this book is available from the British Library

Published by Ladybird Books Ltd
80 Strand London WC2R 0RL
A Penguin Company

001

© Ladybird Books Ltd MMXIV

ISBN: 978-0-72327-104-8

Printed in China